Echoes of The Journey

A COLLECTION OF SHORT STORIES ON

THE ROAD TO PEACE AND PURPOSE

Susie Kirk-Bones

i

Echoes of The Journey

A COLLECTION OF SHORT STORIES ON
THE ROAD TO PEACE AND PURPOSE

Susie Kirk-Bones

DEDICATION

To God be The Glory!

This book is dedicated to:

- My son, Anthony, for his unwavering, unconditional love, which has been my anchor.
- My husband, Joseph, whose simple yet powerful words of encouragement — "You can do it" — gave me the strength to persevere.
- Every dreamer out there, may this book inspire you never to give up.

ACKNOWLEDGMENTS

To Dr. Tonya Williams, your unwavering belief in me, your guidance, and your gentle yet persistent encouragement helped me see potential in myself that I couldn't see on my own. Your impact on my life has been profound, and I am forever grateful.

To my editor, Mr. Kelly, thank you for your relentless dedication and faith. The endless homework, your patience, and the belief that it would all come to pass made this book a reality.

To Vivian, Alfreda, Avis, and Petal, my dear friends and personal cheerleaders, your unwavering support and encouragement have meant everything to me along the way. You lifted me when I needed it the most, and for that, I am deeply grateful.

TABLE OF CONTENTS

INTRODUCTION

There are moments in life when your soul whispers, "Write it down." These moments are not for recognition, not for applause, but because something inside you knows the story must be told.

This book—*Echoes of the Journey*—is my whisper to the world.

It's not a single story with a neat beginning, middle, and end. It's a collection of pieces—snapshots from my life, reflections from my spirit, and characters who might look a lot like your cousin, your neighbor, or maybe even yourself. These stories came to me like unexpected visitors: some appeared during quiet morning walks, others in memories that tugged at my heart, and a few moments when all I could do was whisper, "Jesus, help me."

I didn't plan to share all of this. I was content with the quiet healing that comes from writing for

1

yourself. But the more I wrote, the more I realized—this wasn't just for me.

Each story in this book holds a little piece of truth wrapped in imagination. Some are rooted in my own life. Others are inspired by people I've met, things I've seen, and prayers I've prayed. But all of them carry echoes of laughter, sorrow, strength, questions, and grace.

I invite you to step into the quiet wonder of *The Little House*, where a simple picture frame becomes a doorway into peace, motherhood, and purpose. Walk the track with me in *My Morning Walk* and see how the ordinary can shift into the extraordinary when your imagination walks with God. Sit with the grief and strength of family in *Momma, Can You Hear Me?*, and feel the ache and beauty of coming home in *You Can Never Go "Home" Again*.

Each part of this book—Reflection & The Search for Peace, Trials & Transformation, and Redemption & Purpose—is a season. And, like any season, there are storms and sunshine. There are days when all you can do is endure, and there are days when joy sneaks up on you.

In this book, you'll meet characters like Codi, Emily, and UU, each on their path but all seeking something more profound. You'll hear sirens, feel the breeze of early morning light, and maybe, just maybe, see your reflection tucked between these lines.

This book is my first, and if I'm being honest, it feels a bit like stepping outside without a coat— vulnerable. But I trust that God wouldn't nudge me to open this door if He didn't already know who needed to walk through it.

So, reader, welcome.

Welcome to my journey. Welcome to the stories that made me laugh, cry, pause, and praise. Welcome to moments that might remind you of your own.

As you read, I pray that something echoes in you—a memory, a feeling, a quiet nudge of The Holy Spirit. I hope you find healing in these pages. I hope you find truth. But more than anything, I hope you feel *seen*.

We are all walking stories. And this book? This book is simply mine, shared with love, in case someone out there is waiting for the courage to share theirs.

Thank you for reading. Thank you for listening.

Let the journey begin.

PART 1

REFLECTION & THE SEARCH FOR PEACE

I've always believed that sometimes God speaks the loudest in the quietest moments—through the sound of birds in the morning, a memory that lingers, or a still voice in the middle of a long walk. These first few stories were written during seasons when I wasn't trying to impress anyone. I was just trying to breathe.

I didn't plan for them to be shared. I wrote them because I had to. They helped me rest. They helped me heal.

This part of the journey is about remembering. It's about listening to the echoes of the past—not to get stuck there, but to learn something from it. Like I said once, *"If I cross a bridge that I've crossed before, I know not to step the same way this time."*

These echoes help us see things clearly. They teach us how to walk with more care and more courage.

So, whether you're walking through grief or sitting still with your thoughts, I hope you find something familiar in these pages.

THE LITTLE HOUSE

As she sipped her coffee at the dining room table, she stared at the picture of the little house on the wall. "What a beautiful sight," she thought.

She continued, "It looks so peaceful and quiet and is full of the beauty of nature. Look at the small stream, the large oak tree, and I'm sure the pines whistle and sing a song when the wind blows through them—all the beautiful colors of the flowers seem to blanket the meadow beyond the house."

She took another sip of coffee and thought, "I can imagine the smell of those roses, and oh, how I would like to have those honeysuckles gracing my backyard."

While sitting in her chair at the table, she turned from the picture and took another sip of coffee.

She began to reminisce about her past. Many of her childhood dreams were unfulfilled. Sure, many of them were pretty wild, but attainable.

She laughs silently at some of her mistakes while sending heart-felt praises to God, who cared for her and brought her through.

She then turned her head to look at the picture again and thought, "I wonder what's in that picture I find myself drawn to?" She stares at the picture, looking deeply, and then transposes into it. At first, she is frightened and puzzled. "What's going on? What's happening? Am I really here?" are the questions she asks herself.

She walks up to the porch, takes a seat in the rocking chair, and soon realizes that she has become a part of the painting, but more importantly, that she's feeling a sense of peace and quietness. Likewise, all the other things she was wondering about as she sat quietly, sipping her coffee and staring at the picture, became her reality. She's a part of the painting. She then closes her eyes and inhales the fragrance of the flowers near her. She opens them to the sound of the birds chirping their happy songs. Slowly, the cares of the day leave her mind as she becomes one with nature and its beauty.

She says, "Oh, what a beautiful sight to behold: all of God's creations embracing me." As she looks across the prairie, she sees the crisp blue sky above her and hears the sound of the running stream beside her, all the magic beneath her surrounded by the fresh air that only God can provide.

The Lord speaks to us in all His creations and embraces us unconditionally with love.

As she continues to rest and take in the day, the night draws near, and there's a chill in the air. As the evening transforms into night, the night brings on another joy of its own.

She said, "Look at the many stars that brighten the night sky. The moon shines in glory, and is that the sound of the night bird? *Ole* Mr. Owl? Is that you? So shy but yet so stern." She's still amazed by the peace she feels and the awesomeness of God's handiwork.

She considers it a blessing to experience all of this. It's taken for granted by so many.

Sleep takes over her while she attempts to count the stars. Hours later, she's awakened by the smell of rain and a cool morning breeze. "Could it get any better?" she asks herself.

There's no thought of what she left behind, only excitement of what lies ahead.

She imagines seeing herself dancing across the prairie without a care in the world.

As the morning sky appears, she stands and walks down the steps off the porch and stands on the grass-filled front yard. She says, "There's nothing like a summer shower to refresh this garden of paradise."

She begins to walk among the flowers. With each step she makes, there's more beauty to behold. Oh, how she wishes she could stay forever, but it's time to face reality again.

She sat down in the rocking chair again on the porch, looking around at all the beauty and feeling a peace that words could never explain. The childhood dream of being a writer, a nurse, a songstress, and an explorer all came to mind. She took one last look and remembered what had just taken place, closed her eyes, and opened them only to find herself at the dining room table. The coffee is now cold, but her little house experience will last a lifetime.

It not only made her thankful but also reminded her of the importance of her job as a mom.

Life can get pretty hectic at times, throwing a person off onto an emotional rollercoaster while doubts and unworthiness cloud their God-given purpose. Yet, this visit has cleared her vision, reunited her faith, and restored her purpose.

She finally realized that those childhood dreams of being a writer, a songstress, an explorer, and a nurse had come true in the form of being a mother, the most important job in the world.

When she sees her kids, she's reminded of the beauty of each flower and its fragrance; the strong oak tree reminds her of her husband, and the whispering pines remind her of the fun and laughter they share as a family.

MY MORNING WALK

It was early morning, and the birds were chirping away at my window, announcing, "It's time to get up." So, I opened my eyes, rolled out of my comfortable bed, and thought about what I was going to wear for my usual walk around the high school track.

I thought to myself, "Today seems special in some ways." Then, it dawned on me that this morning was the first time I had been excited to get up and see what the new day had to bring.

I put on the perfect outfit for walking: a blue short-sleeved cotton top, black capri leggings, black ankle socks, and white New Balance sneakers.

While walking towards the door, I saw myself in the full-length mirror. I felt great about myself, and my outfit made me feel even happier. The joy made me say to myself, "I'm ready for my one-mile walk around the track."

Upon arriving at the school track, two ladies dressed like twins in red jogging suits and white sneakers, with red sweatbands around their heads, were walking. As I walked up to the track, they passed by, and we were cordial with each other.

Then, I looked to my left and right and stepped onto the track. With those first few steps, a gentle, cool, refreshing breeze brushed my face as if nature greeted me. It was the kind of air that made you want to breathe deeply, filling your lungs with the purity of the early hour.

As I walked around the track and looked up, I was surrounded by a blanket of stars still shining as the sun crept in for the day. The stars were sitting almost motionless as the moon glowed like a quiet sentinel, casting its gentle light over the gentle morning glow. After that first lap, I thought to myself, "Wow!" I felt my imagination starting to flow.

As I started my second lap around the track, my imagination settled. The red brick high school building, with its three stories, windows trimmed in silver, a tar-paved courtyard, and sidewalks, now became a winding forest trail lined with towering trees with leaves whispering in the morning breeze.

As I continued to walk around, the streetlights morphed into tall, glowing mushrooms, casting a soft, otherworldly glow beneath the canopy of my imagined woodland. Progressing along, the bleachers, once enclosed by the gated fence, were now a small lake that sparkled in the dawn light, with its gentle ripples mirroring the soft hues of the awakening sky. As I made my turn around the track, that ole corner deli with the smell of bacon, eggs, and burnt toast every morning had now become a small quaint cottage, its stone chimney releasing wisps of smoke that carried the comforting aroma of freshly baked bread, inviting passersby to linger in its warm embrace.

On the next lap, far across the road, was a Walgreens store, and now, in its place, nestled in the clearing, was a small village of log cabins with their wooden walls glowing softly in the morning light. And far down the street, where an old, abandoned building once stood, was a small three-room farmhouse with a slanted roof and a hay-filled barn. I was just in time to see the old farmer, dressed in his denim overalls and straw hat, walk toward the barn; I gave him a wave "hello," and he smiled in return. I heard the cows mooing, so he was probably going to milk them or feed them.

During previous walks, I often saw flocks of birds sitting on the wire above the old, abandoned building. And just for a moment, I would watch them fly into different formations above me and return to the wire. They were always coordinated without a miss. But that morning, that old building was gone, and there was no wire for them to sit. I thought, "Where are they now?" My imagination was stirred as I turned the corner of yet another lap, and I began to see the birds flying all around in those fantastic formations, and taking a moment to sit on the farmhouse's slanted roof.

Did I mention there was a flock of geese that fed on the grassy lawn? I saw them, too, as I walked. They were not as unified as the birds, but seeing them waddle and hearing their strange sound amazed me.

Suddenly, as I continued to walk and allow my imagination to be free, I realized that my next lap around the track would be my last. I wanted to see the last segment of the sunrise in the eastern sky and witness the many shades of color it creates across the morning sky.

Remember the birds on that slanted roof? Well, the morning sky made them come alive as they gracefully danced in flight, painting the heavens with their movements, shifting seamlessly between patterns. Some birds formed a perfect V shape, while others weaved into intricate shapes like nature's calligraphy. Their wings caught the soft glow of the rising sun, scattering golden light with every beat. The air was filled with their melodious calls, harmonizing with the gentle rustle of the breeze as if orchestrating a symphony to celebrate the new day.

So, my imaginary scenery around the school track had ended along with my walk. I could hear the conversations with the many people who had joined the track begin to rise above the natural sounds of nature.

The two ladies I saw earlier, dressed like twins, came over to ask me, "What are you staring at?"

I smiled, pointed my finger to the sky, and said, "Look up."

"Don't you see the shades of color the sun comes in before it reaches its peak?" I explained.

"Have you noticed the flock of birds that fly over in different formations before they perch on the wires, not to mention those geese over there?" as I paused and looked. Then I said, "And as you started this morning, did you notice that the air was fresh and crisp, unlike what you will smell after the traffic starts?"

As I looked at the two ladies, they looked at me as if I was off, but I was too engulfed in the reality of life.

I continued, "This morning, outside my window, I could hear the chirping of morning birds saying, 'Get up.'"

The ladies smiled at me, and one said, "What was in your coffee this morning?" As I walked away, I turned around, smiled, and said, "Jesus."

MOMMA, CAN YOU HEAR ME?

On a dreary, overcast day, we followed the hearse to New Canaan Baptist Church—the church we cherished as kids.

The wooden floors creaked beneath our feet as we walked down the aisle. The sun shone through the stained-glass windows, which caused a glow with warm hues. We saw the towering pulpit surrounded by five chairs and the organ that played hymns every Sunday.

As I reflect, Saturday nights were always spent preparing for Sunday services. Mom pressed and styled the girls' hair, ironed their dresses, shined the boys' shoes, and sometimes made them wear ties. I was relieved when she stopped using white shirts—they never stayed clean anyway.

There were nine of us—six girls and three boys—and Mom managed us well, often with just a look.

As I reminisce about my childhood, I feel the bittersweetness of this moment. Church was her place to find strength, encouragement, and the company of old friends. Her faith in God gave her and us a foundation of stability. We never lacked what mattered. Sure, we wanted the material things other kids had, but we had each other, and we had lots of love. We didn't need the newest toys or fancy games. We made up our own, and with so many of us, fun was never in short supply.

Momma's home was the heart of the neighborhood. All the kids would come over and play, and Mom always had treats for everyone.

My dad was the quiet type. He didn't have to say much to get his point across. My sisters' male friends were intimidated by him, but they adored my mom.

Daddy wasn't mean—just serious and not the social type. He worked long hours to provide for us, while Momma picked up side jobs to supplement the income.

When it came to discipline, Momma gave the lecture, and Daddy delivered the punishment. A switch, a belt, sometimes even two switches—those were his tools. He'd always say, "You'll thank me one day," or "This hurts me more than it hurts you." How could it hurt him more than us when we were the ones in pain?

As kids, we didn't understand. But now, I get it. I think we all do. We each said "thank you" in our way. The discipline gave us respect, values, self-worth, strength, morals, and above all, faith in The Almighty God.

Yes, those were good times. And now, here we are again—not happy like we were at the family reunions or family gatherings—this time, to say "so long" to Momma. We each have different careers, and we've each failed at something, but she always reminded us, and I quote, "What don't kill you will make you stronger." My mom, the philosopher.

I recall being in a difficult relationship. I wanted her to say, "Leave. Come home." But she just listened, occasionally saying a few words to remind me she was still on the line. When I finished pouring out my heart, she said calmly, "You've already made your mind up. You just needed an ear." At the time, I didn't know what to make of that. But as I grew older, I understood—she was letting me own my choices. If I failed, it was mine to learn from.

Momma, can you hear me? I want to share something with you. I need your listening ears.

Tears rolled down my cheeks as we sat before her casket. She was dressed in all white, like the angel she was and will always be. Flowers rested gently on each side of her, with their sweet aroma enveloping us.

As I looked quietly around at my siblings and extended family, I knew each of them was remembering their special moment with Momma. Even my father—the quiet one—had tears streaming down his face, twenty-five years of marriage. Good times, bad times. Through sickness and health. 'Til death do us part. This parting was painful for us all.

But I hear you, Momma, saying: "God will see you through."

Thinking of the funeral service, my mind flashed back:

> "I remember my first day of school. She cried. 'Momma, why are you crying?' I asked. She said, 'My first boy is growing up, and soon you'll leave the nest.' She told me I was the second man of the house. She told me, 'Look after your sisters and your younger

brothers. Make me proud.' That was the only time I ever saw my Momma cry. I promised myself I'd never be the cause of her tears again."

One by one, we grew up and set out into the world. And every time, she was there—hugs, best wishes, and silent prayers. I know she cried on some nights, missing us. I know she prayed for God to watch over us, to keep His hand on our lives.

As I continued to reflect, I recall:

"I joined the military after high school—wanted to make her proud. We spoke on the phone every week and exchanged letters and care packages frequently. Traveling from state to state was an adventure, but my favorite memories were always from being home. Seeing her and the 'crew' made every visit worthwhile, though leaving again was always hard.

If I stayed stateside, I know Momma was relieved—and so was I. But in the Army, nothing is set in stone. We heard rumors of deployment to the Gulf War, but again, nothing was certain.

Four years passed. I'd become used to this Army life: be ready, be alert, be focused, be fit. One day, the Unit called a meeting. We were scheduled to join another company headed to Iraq.

So far away from you, not knowing how long I'll be there...

Okay, I hear you, Momma. I heard you saying, 'God will take care of you.' I said, 'I'll call you when I get settled.' And just like that, off I went.

Adjusting to new climates, new food, a different language, and unfamiliar faces was one thing. But nothing prepared me for the sound of gunfire or the silence of not hearing from loved ones.

I recall I promised not to make her cry.

I told her, 'Today, I fired at my first target. I don't know if I hit it or missed.' So many questions, so many sleepless nights, wounded friends, and destruction all around.

I asked myself, 'Why am I here?' While telling myself, 'I won't cry, I just want to vent.' Then, I would remember her say,

'You're in God's hands and always in my prayers.'

Back on the road again with another Unit, we got hit by an IED. The blast injured me and three of my buddies. How could I tell Momma? I promised I'd never make her cry. From our letters, I think she knew. She never asked. I never said.

A year after the injury, I returned stateside, stationed in Georgia. Once I settled in, I drove to Alabama to surprise her. I could already see her smile in my mind. That four-hour drive was fueled by the thought of seeing her face when I walked through the door.

But the surprise was on me.

The house was empty and still. Before I could grab my key, Mrs. Fannie, our longtime neighbor, rushed over.

Her voice shook as she said, 'They took your Momma to the hospital last night. It's serious.' 'Serious?' I thought as I jumped back in the car. 'What could it be? She never mentioned anything to me, and if she told my siblings, I am sure they would have told me.'

25

Momma's favorite words were, 'I'm fine, don't worry, God is good.'

That's how she was—she didn't want us to worry.

I rushed to the hospital and made it just in time. Her eyes were dim. I saw pain in her face, but she tried to mask it with a faint smile. She motioned me over and, in a whisper, said, 'I love you. I am so proud of you. I asked God to let me see you one more time—and He did.'

Tears rolled down my cheeks. 'I love you, my Queen,' I said.

She squeezed my hand, and then her eyes closed for the last time. The doctor informed us that her heart had been bad for some time, and there was nothing they could do. You can imagine the questions that flooded my head, but her answer would always be, 'Don't worry, I'm in God's hands.'

One more hug. One more word of encouragement. That's all I want today. But here I sit, not ready to say goodbye."

The choir begins to sing "Precious Lord,"[1] her favorite song—and I lose control. I tried to be strong. I wanted to be strong. But the pain is too much.

Momma, can you hear me?

I'm sorry. I'm not strong today. We all miss you so much. We all hear you.

The choir sings on:

"Through the storm, through the night,
Lead me on to the light,
Take my hand, precious Lord, lead me home.
Hear my cry, hear my call,
Hold my hand lest I fall,
Take my hand, precious Lord, lead me home."

Rest well, Momma. We'll be strong for one another.

The foundation has already been laid.

---

[1] "PRECIOUS LORD, TAKE MY HAND." *Digital Songs & Hymns*, digitalsongsandhymns.com/songs/4123.

YOU CAN NEVER GO "HOME" AGAIN

After living in a rehabilitation center in the big city for 17 years, Codi was now 36 and finally able to return home to the life he loved. He felt much better, although his memory was still a little spotty at times.

Being from a small town, he enjoyed the peace and quiet. He also enjoyed the many hellos and smiles he received from the townspeople he called family. He missed the Sunday gatherings before and after church. He missed the old hymns, praises, and heartfelt worship during church hours. But most of all, he missed that divine connection he felt every time he walked through the neighborhood.

Now, arriving back home after being away for 17 years, he felt alone, isolated, and forgotten. The town had changed. A liquor store had replaced the barber shop where his dad took him to get his first haircut. The mom-and-pop stores on the left side of the street had turned into a large department store. The town square—where people met for holiday celebrations, shaded by a large oak tree near the benches, beside the wildflower garden—was now just a memory. His walk through the town had become a scene from a magazine: beautiful but untouchable.

He sat on his porch many days, watching the days turn into nights while asking God, "What's happened to my home? Where are the families? Nobody knows anybody anymore. They walk past you with no greetings, not even a smile. Could I have been gone that long, or am I living in a nightmare?"

He had only been home for a week and instantly noticed the change, but was still looking forward to Sunday morning services. He told himself that times were changing, people were busier, and kids had grown up. But that ole divine connection with The Lord still remained in the hearts of his hometown family, and Sunday service would prove that.

Codi recalled the times when his father would take him to church. He remembered how Mom was the first to leave the house because she sang in the choir. Then he and Pop would arrive just in time for The

Word. He thought to himself, "I really miss those days of my youth—and the many times we'd stop at the ice cream parlor after service was over."

Codi got up early Sunday morning, thanked God for another day, and sang praises as he waited for the time to leave. He felt so good walking the three blocks to the church, greeting everyone on the way with a big smile and a cheerful, "Good to see you!"

When he finally reached the church entrance, he noticed that the pastor wasn't at the door to greet everyone. The parking lot didn't have as many cars as usual, and no kids were running around.

"What is going on?" he asked himself as he slowly walked up the church steps and into the building.

As he removed his hat, he looked around and took in all the changes that had taken place in the sanctuary. The pulpit now resembled a stage, with strobe lights beaming from the ceiling. There was no choir stand; instead, monitors were positioned on both sides of the church. And what happened to the organ? Drums and keyboards now stood centered in the background.

Slowly walking to a seat near the altar, a little boy— no more than eight years old—touched his hand, gave him a big smile, and said, "Welcome, sir."

Codi's eyes filled with tears of joy. For the first time since he'd arrived home, he was greeted with kindness.

The service began with prayer, scripture, and songs. Codi prayed silently, asking God to help him not judge or compare what was happening today to the times before. After all, time changes a lot of things, including traditions.

As he sat quietly listening, he prayed again—this time hoping that an old hymn would be sung so that he could join in. But no hymn was sung.

The preacher stepped up to the podium, holding what looked like a phone to Codi, but it was actually a tablet. Codi looked around for a Bible near his seat to follow along with the scripture, but he couldn't find one. A lady noticed him looking around and asked if she could be of any help.

"Where are The Bibles?" he whispered.

She pointed to the monitor on the wall, smiled, and said, "We don't use them anymore."

Codi sat back, his mind going a mile a minute, trying to take in all the changes that had taken place in God's house.

After church, he yearned to talk with someone and decided to invite an old friend over for tea and conversation. But as he looked around the congregation, there were no familiar faces. He also noticed that the service was quick, with no mention of salvation, but with repeated reminders to sow a seed, donate to the building fund, and support upcoming events.

Codi was shocked, to say the least.

As he stood there after dismissal, looking over the congregation, he thought, "What has happened to the hearts of God's people? My family? My friends?"

He left the church more confused, empty, and angrier than he had ever felt in a long time.

As he walked back to his home, the little boy he had met earlier ran up to walk alongside him.

"Mister, what's wrong? Are you feeling okay?" asked the little boy.

Codi looked down and said, "You're too young to understand the hurt I'm feeling right now, but thanks for asking."

The little boy said, "My name is Greene."

"Greene? Your name is Greene?" asked Codi.

"Yes," the little boy said. "My grandmother told me green is life, and I brought life into her world."

Codi was surprised to hear such words from this little boy's mouth.

"My name is Codi. Do you live in this neighborhood?" he asked.

Greene pointed to the house across the street with a bed of roses planted near the gate.

"I live there with my grandmother. Where do you live, Mr. Codi?"

Codi replied, "Well, it seems like I am three houses from you, but on the opposite side."

They both shared a smile, and Greene invited Codi over for a cool glass of iced tea and to meet his grandmother.

Codi accepted.

Greene ran up to the door shouting, "Grandma! Grandma! I hope you have some good ole iced tea ready, 'cause I have a friend with me!"

Grandma was accustomed to Greene shouting and his invisible friends visiting on Sundays. But this time, when she looked out the window, she was shocked to see that there was a man with him. She greeted them at the door.

"Come in, sir. Everyone calls me Grandma, but my name is Joy," she said.

"And my name is Codi. I hope I'm not intruding on your Sunday," he replied.

"Nonsense," she said. "I'm glad to meet a friend of my grandson, Greene."

While Codi and Grandma were getting to know each other, Greene came in with iced tea and a big smile on his face.

"See, Grandma? I do have a friend!"

They all sat around sipping iced tea, telling jokes, sharing stories, and bonding. Codi felt at home again. He wanted to ask Joy about the changes that had taken place in the neighborhood, but decided not to—he didn't want to spoil the warm feeling he was experiencing.

The three of them laughed and sang some old hymns that Codi had longed to hear. Soon, it was time for him to leave, but he promised to visit again.

Before turning in for the night, he prayed and thanked God for an unusual but glorious day.

After a good night's sleep, Codi was awakened by birds singing outside his window. As his feet touched the floor, a large smile came over his face, followed by joy in his heart.

Codi thought, "Even the birds sing praises to God. What a wonderful God we serve."

The day began with praise to The Holy Father and a reminder of yesterday's church service.

As Codi thought about the differences in his church experience from previous years to the present, he tried to put them out of his mind, but something kept nagging at him. He remembered—the church hadn't been full like it was in the past. The songs felt more secular (contemporary gospel, as it was now called). The praise and worship experience was minimal, and everyone seemed to be on a tight schedule, rushing to get out.

Codi pondered the thoughts in his mind, repeatedly trying to piece it all together without judging. He just wanted to know what had changed the family-oriented church he remembered.

As the day drew to a close, he decided to take a walk through the neighborhood—this time venturing into a different part of town. He hoped he had simply overlooked an area that still felt the same as before.

Maybe, just maybe, he would find some answers to the questions that lingered in his heart—questions about why that divine connection seemed to have vanished from the hearts of the people he once called family.

Walking around the neighborhood, looking at old buildings, new stores, new additions—and to his surprise, more liquor stores and a gambling hall where the old playground once was—sent shockwaves down his spine.

"So this is change?!" he yelled. "Good things replaced by evil."

As he walked closer to home, he heard laughter coming from Ms. Joy's house. What a wonderful sound to hear after walking through a gloomy neighborhood. Greene saw him coming and ran out to meet him, giving him a big smile and a warm hug. Codi was surprised and thankful that they had met.

Greene started questioning Codi about his walk, but before Codi could answer, they had reached the gate to Mrs. Joy's home. She asked him to come in for another cool glass of iced tea. And again, the three of them picked up from where they left off.

After that day, Codi made it a habit to take a daily walk, determined to find an old friend to inquire about the changes. He really didn't want to ask Mrs. Joy, but decided he would the next time they met.

It had been a busy week for Codi. With one more day left before another Sunday service, he decided to catch up on his reading.

Before Codi entered rehabilitation, he had arranged for a housekeeper to maintain his home. She had done an excellent job caring for the place in his absence, keeping the interior spotless and ensuring the lawn was always well-manicured.

One thoughtful thing she had done was save some of the local newspapers. She hadn't kept all of them, only those that covered major news about the town. Most of the articles highlighted new businesses opening in the area, rezoning updates, and newly appointed officials.

She had hoped that keeping those papers would help Codi readjust when he returned. But after reading through them, he found himself even more frustrated. The articles didn't answer his questions; if anything, they raised more. He even began writing them down.

As the week drew to a close, Codi looked forward to Sunday service and another opportunity to visit with Greene and Mrs. Joy.

Sunday morning service was just like before—except this time, he was able to join in and sing an old hymn.

Greene was there and invited him over for Sunday dinner. Little did he know this would be the dinner that would answer his questions—and open some painful wounds.

On their way to Grandma's house, Greene noted that Codi was silent, with a look of sadness on his face. He felt bad and offered to help by listening if Codi wanted to talk.

Codi looked down at Greene and said, "Thanks, but I'm afraid you're too young to understand."

Greene said, "I may be young, Mr. Codi, but you are my friend—and I wanna help you." He paused, then added, "It's the church, isn't it?"

Codi looked surprised. "Why do you say that?"

"Because I've noticed you in church, and afterward. You're always sad. What makes you so sad after you leave church, Mr. Codi?"

Codi could do nothing but give him a false smile and a pat on the head.

"Such wisdom and sensitivity from a young lad," he thought.

By this time, Codi and Greene reached Grandma's house, and Grandma Joy had come to the door.

"Well, come on in, you two. Did Greene talk your head off again, Mr. Codi?" she asked.

Before Codi could answer, Greene said, "No, Grandma. He's troubled over the service at church. Can you help him? He says I'm too young to understand."

Grandma smiled and said, "Not before dinner. Food makes everyone feel better, talk better, and listen better. Come on in, and let's see what we can do to make Mr. Codi feel better. Go wash your hands and get ready for a delicious meal: collard greens, macaroni, and cheese, fried okra, smothered chicken with onion gravy, cornbread, sweet potato casserole, and good ole iced tea."

"Hmm, sounds good," said Greene. "And what's for dessert?"

Grandma said, "Mr. Codi, I hope you like it. For dessert, I have banana pudding in the fridge— Greene's favorite."

"Mrs. Joy…" Codi began, but Grandma cut him off.

"No, call me Grandma."

With a tear in his eye, he said, "Thank you."

Grandma replied, "You are welcome. After dinner, we'll try to answer those questions that make you sad after church. Now, let's eat."

After dinner, the three of them went out to the back porch with iced tea and dessert in hand, ready to discuss what bothered Codi.

He started by thanking Joy for the dinner and the comfort of her home, but mainly for Greene, her little grandson with the big heart.

"Grandma," Codi began, "I don't know where to start. I guess I should start with me."

"I've lived in this town all my life—except for the 17 years I spent in rehab. But before I went to rehab, I owned a small hardware store. My days were spent in that store, and my nights were spent home alone. Oh, how I longed to be a part of a loving family— but there was only me. Mom and Dad died at an early age in an automobile crash, and I didn't know at the time that my mother was pregnant with a child. A little brother or sister for me."

"I was 14 at the time. Too young to manage a store, but with my uncle's help, we did fine. When I finished high school, at the age of 17, he told me we had to sell the store because business wasn't good and there wouldn't be enough money to continue my education. So, two months later, the store was sold, and I stayed in the house trying to figure out what the rest of my life would look like."

"Uncle Joe suggested that we move to a larger town with more opportunities, but my heart was here— Hartsville, Maryland. So, after a year, we parted ways. I started working as a chef at a café near the expressway. There, I met a lot of travelers and people from my hometown whom I adopted as family. Going to work felt like going to hang out with loved ones. Those were the days I treasured."

"There was one lady who reminded me of my mom, so I hired her as my housekeeper. She was motherly," he smiled.

Then Codi said, "Then something happened that changed my life completely."

He turned to Grandma and paused. "Grandma, should I continue? It gets sad for me as the memories come back."

Grandma smiled and gently motioned for Codi to continue. "Codi, whatever it is, now is the time to reclaim what you lost."

Codi bowed his head. "Okay, I guess you're right. Now let's see... oh yeah, the thing that changed my life."

"Well, one rainy night, I was asked to work late. The café was busy—people stopping in to get some hot food and drink and to pass the time until the rain let up. I remember the jukebox playing oldies, and everyone was just having fun, like at a family reunion, and I was right in the middle of it all. Then, one by one, they left as the rain let up, with full stomachs, joyful hearts, and smiles that could light up the darkest sky. It was one of the best nights of my life."

"And then it happened…"

"Three men came in just as I was about to close for the evening. They were drunk, yelling, waving a gun, and asking for money. I tried to reason with them, but the alcohol had control of their minds."

"I didn't know a young lady was in the bathroom until she came out. Before I could say anything, the gunman shot her, and they ran out of the café."

"Grandma, I tried to do CPR on her while I waited for the ambulance and police. In minutes, they were there. I prayed that the woman would make it."

"After I gave my statement to the officers, I asked if I could go to the hospital to check on her. I didn't know her name or where she was from. All I knew was—she was family, and I needed to be there. But they didn't let me go."

"After that, the café was closed for further investigation, which gave me time to visit the young lady. I called her Angel. I never did find out her real name. The doctors gave me encouraging news each time I visited her, but she was in a coma, unable to give them any information. No family came—not that I saw."

"Then, one day, they told me they didn't think she would make it through the night. That's when I lost it. Another tragedy in my life. My family... I blamed myself for not being strong, not handing over the money, not stopping the gunman... everything."

"The doctors tried to console me, but the grief was just too much. I was young but had already lost so much—my parents, the family business, my uncle leaving me, and now this botched robbery. I spiraled. I had a nervous breakdown right there in the hospital."

"So, the doctors and staff admitted me into rehab. The rest is in bits and pieces—I don't remember spending any time at home after that."

"I remember staring into a doctor's face, and he was asking me, 'Do you know who you are?' He told me I had collapsed in the hospital, unresponsive, with a touch of amnesia. I tried so hard to remember everything, but it was all a blank. He assured me that, in time, I would have a full recovery. And for the last 17 years, I've been in a rehabilitation center under the care of Dr. Smith."

Grandma was silent for a moment. Then she spoke gently.

"Codi, I understand what you are feeling, and I see why family is so important. But you shouldn't blame yourself or carry the past hurts into your present. If you do, you'll destroy your chance for a fulfilling future."

Codi nodded. "Dr. Smith said pretty much the same thing—that I need to break down the wall if I want to let others in. But when I returned, I tried to get that ole feeling again, only to find out things and people have changed."

He sighed. "The church is one thing I thought would be the same, and it hurts me to think that people don't care about each other anymore. I've walked this neighborhood, greeted and smiled at everyone I met—and the only one who smiled back was your grandson. He is true to his name."

"Am I trying to live in the past if I want love in the present? Joy, laughter, fun, getting along, and just enjoying life? Grandma, are my expectations too high?"

"You know... I never knew the name of that young girl who was shot. I wish I could tell her family how sorry I am."

After a short sob, Codi continued, "Thanks, Grandma, for caring and listening. I hope I didn't wear out my welcome."

"You are welcome to drop by anytime," she said warmly.

Then she stood, went into the house, refilled the iced tea glasses, and returned with an old newspaper clipping. She handed it to Codi and said, "Read this. Maybe it will answer some of your questions and put your soul at ease."

The article named the girl Sandra Mackenzie. She hadn't died as a result of the robbery, but had remained in the hospital in a coma for three months.

Just when the doctors had nearly given up, she opened her eyes and smiled.

As Codi read a few paragraphs, he gasped and dropped the newspaper.

Grandma said, "Though the bullet caused damage to her back, she eventually recovered. The town mourned for months over the loss of the café and the young man known for his smile and generous heart. People grew up. Some left town. Others remained in their comfort zones. And the town became what you see now."

"What about the church?" Codi asked.

Grandma replied, "Codi, the church is people. I suppose they felt that God was not listening—or that He had abandoned them in their sadness. Anyway, life goes on."

She looked at him intently and said, "Have you ever heard the old saying, 'You can never go home again?' Well, it's true. Once you leave, changes start to happen, and you notice them more when you return than if you had stayed. But don't let those changes change you. Bring back the joy you once had and share it with the people you have now."

"A part of this town may have died—but you didn't. Don't you think it's time to bury the dead and start living?" she asked.

They both smiled, and Codi said, "You're right."

Then he asked, "One more question... Did Sandra, the young lady, live near here? And does she still have any family around that I could speak to?"

Grandma smiled and called into the house, "Greene! Come out to the porch, baby."

As Greene came outside, Grandma said, "This is Greene—Sandra's son. And if the mailbox weren't so rusty, you'd see the name Mackenzie. Sandra was my daughter. After she came out of the hospital, it took time before she could walk, but she eventually did. She went back to school, returned to work, met a nice young man, and married him. He's in the military, so they travel a lot."

"I was thrilled for her—and even happier when she told me she was pregnant. She had the baby in Germany. They stayed there for a year and then came back here for a while. Greene was only 18 months old when his father received orders to leave for China. Of course, I was thrilled when they asked me to keep him. He was such a good baby. With a name like William Wilson Thomas, named after his father, he had to be special. So I nicknamed him Greene," she smiled.

Codi could do nothing but give her a big hug—with tears streaming down his face—and say, "I'm so sorry."

Grandma returned the hug—and so did Greene.

She went on, "My daughter often spoke of the café and always came home with a smile and tons of stories that made me laugh. During the investigation, the officers eventually found her ID in the ladies' room. It must have fallen out of her purse. They notified me, and you can imagine the rest. I was so worried when I didn't hear from her. I was out of town when everything happened, and I couldn't get back right away because I was traveling overseas."

"You were probably under sedation or already moved to the rehab center when I returned to town."

"We didn't know where you were or if you'd ever come back. Even in a small town, who would have guessed that the man who helped my daughter, lived just a few houses down? But it was in God's plan for us to meet," said Grandma, looking at him with kind, steady eyes.

Then she added, "I hope your mind is at ease, because God knows I am at peace just by hearing you share what really happened that night. And I want you to know that you are family. And we welcome you."

PART 2

TRIALS & TRANSFORMATION

I'll be honest with you—this part wasn't easy to write. But life isn't always easy.

Some of these stories came during seasons when I felt invisible, when I battled doubt, or when my mind was too tired even to put words on paper. I remember a time when I had a mental block. I felt creativity, and I was trying to pull it out. But nothing would come. Then, The Lord said to me to rest.

These pages hold what came after the rest. They're about storms I didn't see coming and truths I didn't know I needed. There's some imagination in here, sure—but underneath that, there's reality, struggle, lessons, and transformation.

This section is for anyone who has been in the midst of the mess and didn't know how to pray except to whisper, *"Jesus, help me."*

We don't always get answers right away, but transformation often begins in those hard places. If you're in one of those places now, hold on. You're not alone.

I CAN STILL HEAR THE SIRENS

Loving memories faded in and out as I wrote this story. Smiles and joy fluttered in my heart, and then I paused a moment—for the sirens—and asked myself why. But then again, why not?

It was Wednesday, March 18, 2020. Something about it felt strange, yet it was just a typical day. My husband and I had appointments with the eye doctor. As usual, we went to IHOP for brunch and then to the local Walmart afterward. There was nothing special to buy; I was just browsing. On days like that, I would always call it our "date day"—quality time together, away from work and the house.

Little did I know that this day would mark the beginning of something I never imagined would happen.

He went to work as usual on Thursday morning—a normal day and night. But Friday morning, when he didn't go to work, was just the beginning of a nightmare.

The day started with a fever and some fatigue. I thought it was just a flu bug—nothing that rest and plenty of fluids couldn't fix. But Saturday came, and the fever was a bit higher; the fatigue lingered. I said, "Just get some rest and food in your stomach, and tomorrow will be a better day."

Tomorrow? A better day? What an understatement.

Sunday morning came with no changes. But there was still no pain, and the fever had gone down a notch. I thought, *I guess it's time to bring on the chicken soup and more fluids.* I told him, "Rest well, honey, and tomorrow will be a better day."

Tomorrow… a better day? I could only hope.

On Monday morning, it was raining outside—a day only the ducks would enjoy. It was the kind of day made for staying inside with a warm cup of tea. Instead, we opted for oatmeal with bananas and juice.

I asked, "Honey, how are you feeling today?"

"The fever is gone, but the fatigue still lingers," he replied.

I thought, *"That ole flu bug must be on its way out. By the end of the day, he'll be feeling much better."*

But the breakfast came up and out no sooner than I finished that thought.

I shouted, "Okay, that's it—we're going to the doctor!"

As my thoughts filled with concern, I asked God, "What is going on with him?"

The rain poured harder, and the wind picked up. *I can still hear the sirens.*

My husband tried to act like all was well, but I could tell he was pretending. He was getting weaker and could barely walk, but we made it to the doctor's office.

At that time, we didn't know he had been exposed to the virus. So when the doctor asked, we said no. She checked him out and found that his sugar was very high. He had an infection and a dry cough. She gave him antibiotics and some cough syrup and stressed that he should take his diabetic medications faithfully. She said he should be okay.

So—in our rationalizing—it was his sugar that was causing all this weakness. I thought, *"Gotta check his sugar often, make sure he's taking the pills, and keep an eye on his diet. I can do that—and he should be better in no time."*

It was Monday night. He ate, took his meds, and was now relaxing in front of MSNBC in his man cave. I was enjoying a movie in the bedroom. All seemed well.

Thank you, Jesus!

When the movie ended, it was nice to hear the rain tapping against the window—a relaxing way to close a stressful day.

By that time, COVID had already claimed many lives. The hospitals were filling up. A shutdown was on the horizon.

"Lord, please help us get through this pandemic," I prayed.

As the rain continued to pour, I heard sirens. *"Where are they?"* I wondered. *"They sound so close,"* I thought. So I concentrated on the sound of the rain as I slowly drifted off to sleep.

It was 2 a.m. Before I could make my way downstairs, he was already coming up, a sad look on his face.

I asked, "Honey, what's wrong?" as I helped him into bed. I felt his forehead—the fever had returned.

"There's no pain, just discomfort. It should go away soon," he said.

As he rolled over to sleep, my mind flooded with questions.

"There's no sleep for me tonight. I have to stay awake and monitor him."

I prayed, *"Lord, what is going on? Are the sirens coming to my home? The devil is a liar! I refuse to entertain that thought."*

He tossed and turned. I got up to give him space to find a comfortable spot. I knew then that there would be no sleep for me. What I didn't realize then was that my nightmare had just begun.

It was Tuesday morning. I got a call from my friend. She told me, "Two church members passed away today." The news reported more deaths from the virus. The hospitals were overrun. They even advised, "Don't call 911 unless it's a real emergency."

And still, I heard more sirens—more than the night before.

Soon, my husband took a turn for the worse. His fever escalated. He had no appetite. He wasn't drinking water. He was hallucinating. He was restless.

Now I was really wondering, *"Does he have the virus?"*

I asked, "Oh Lord, what am I to do?"

I heard in my heart, *"Breathe. Take a breath. It's no time to panic."*

I asked my husband, "Honey, talk to me. Tell me what you want me to do. I'm here."

He gave me a strange look, as if he didn't know who I was, and told me he was okay.

Then he said he needed to use the bathroom. And it was at that moment I realized—he didn't even have the strength to get up. I brought the bedside potty to him. His urine was dark. He was dehydrated.

I told him, "You need to drink some water."

He said, "No."

Now, the war had begun. My husband was no longer my strong husband. He had become like a child, and I had to become both mother and nurse.

I went into the bathroom, got the medicine dropper, and dropped water into his mouth. But that wasn't enough. I went to the kitchen and brought back a cup with a bendable straw. That worked. Thank God.

He lay back down. I returned to the kitchen to make a light breakfast—chicken broth. Thankfully, he ate all of it. He took his meds and let me check his sugar and temperature. Only the sugar was high.

I asked, "Do you know who I am?"

He smiled and said, "Susie."

That made my day.

He was resting, so I prepared dinner for him. So far, so good.

At some point, I lost track of the days. He was in and out of lucidity. I just knew—I now had a child to care for, in every sense of the word.

He was semi-bedridden, so I had to give him sponge baths and keep the potty nearby. Sometimes, he refused to let me help him with the most basic things needed to stay clean and fed.

He would sing during bath time—*"Once a man, twice a child."*

Then one day, he looked at me and said, "I'm no man anymore. I'm a child." And he cried.

He asked, "Honey, am I going to get any better?"

My heart broke, but I had to stay strong. I told him, "It's just a phase. Let me take care of you."

He grew calm again and fell back asleep. I walked into the bathroom, emptied and cleaned the tubs, and let the tears flow down my face.

The next morning, I said to myself, *"It must be a new day."* I couldn't even remember what day it was. But I knew he had rested well, and I had finally gotten some much-needed sleep.

Then came a text from the church: "Two more members have passed away."

This pandemic was taking a toll on the whole world. We were in lockdown. Only essential businesses were open. Grocery and drug stores had long lines. Masks were now required for everyone.

Just when I thought things were improving, life hit again.

He was now having trouble breathing.

I got up early and went to the drugstore. I bought a humidifier and an inhaler. It helped—for a while.

His family called every day to check on him. Sometimes, it was overwhelming, but thanks be to God, He gave me the grace to stay calm and keep my emotions in check.

I can't remember what day it was when the sirens finally stopped at our door. I had to call 911. My husband had told me his breathing was getting worse. As I was helping him get dressed, the doorbell rang—the paramedics had arrived.

I explained everything he had been experiencing. I gave them his medical history.

They looked at me with serious eyes and said it was better to keep him home. "Have him sleep on his left side, keep giving him his meds, and monitor his breathing," they advised. "The hospitals are overcrowded, and honestly, his chances of survival there are slim to none."

Their words hit me hard. But the advice made sense. I followed their instructions—every single day.

Then came a new day. He was feeling much better. His sugar levels were down. The fever was gone. His appetite had returned. He was drinking water again—this time from a glass. But he was frustrated. He still hadn't regained his strength.

I reminded him, "It's a blessing that you've come this far."

I remembered one moment in particular. He was sitting in the bathtub, tears streaming down his face. All I could do was hold him and whisper, "You're going to be all right. One day at a time."

We cried together.

And in that silent moment, I knew in my heart, we would survive this.

Praise be to God.

I see my husband slowly recovering from this nightmare. When I try to explain everything that happened—to him, to us—I get choked up inside. It's only by God's grace that he's still here.

We don't know what tomorrow will bring, and I won't pretend the journey is over. But I can exhale and thank God for keeping us.

"Weeping may endure for a night, but joy comes in the morning." (Psalm 30:5b)

I can still hear the sirens.

THE INK THAT ERASED ME

In a close-knit community where everyone knew each other's names and secrets, the streets were lined with oak trees that whispered secrets in the wind. Children played in the park, and neighbors chatted over white picket fences, sharing stories and laughter. But beneath the idyllic surface, hidden tensions and unspoken rivalries added an air of intrigue.

At Emily's family home, a charming two-story house nestled on the outskirts of town, ivy-covered walls, and a flower-filled garden gave it a storybook feel. The creaky wooden floors and the faint scent of lavender made it feel cozy and lived-in. Yet, within this home, there was a secret. Arguments between Emily's parents, Sue and Joe, continued to grow.

Sue, with her warm smile and nurturing demeanor, made everyone feel at ease. Her long chestnut braids framed a face that was always ready with a kind word or comforting hug. Joe, in contrast, had sharp features and deep-set eyes, often lost in thought. He carried a quiet strength, but the recent arguments had cast a shadow over his once-steady gaze.

Emily, a spirited and imaginative twenty-year-old with a short crop haircut and shiny brown eyes, had always been the curious type, often losing herself in the worlds she created on paper.

In her cluttered bedroom, filled with books, sketches, and empty coffee cups, Emily's pen scratched furiously across the paper as the midnight deadline loomed. With a final flourish, she dotted the last sentence and slumped back in her chair, a sigh of relief escaping her lips. But as she glanced at the page, her heart skipped a beat. The words had vanished.

Bewildered, she turned to the mirror and gasped. Her reflection was gone.

She stood in stunned silence, panic creeping in. She thought, *"What just happened?"*

Emily hadn't done anything different that day. She hadn't eaten anything strange. And yet, her words had vanished—and she had disappeared. Shakily, she sat back down and instinctively clicked the pen in her hand, heart pounding.

Her reflection flickered back into view.

She stared at the pen, then at herself, a mix of confusion and battling fear. She thought, *"What is this thing?"*

Determined to understand what had just happened, she retraced her steps, her mind racing. It didn't take long for her to realize the pen was the key. It had the power to make her invisible, and anything she wrote could disappear along with her.

The discovery was sudden, terrifying, and electrifying all at once. Emily had stumbled into a mystery she couldn't yet explain and an adventure that would change her life forever.

Realizing her power, Emily was overwhelmed by a multitude of questions. She thought, *"What should I do? Who should I tell? Should I use this for myself?"*

The questions swirled, each more pressing than the last.

Undecided, she decided to test the pen again. Holding her breath, she scribbled a few words on a scrap of paper and clicked the pen. Instantly, the words vanished—and so did she. Yet, this time, Emily was prepared.

She moved silently through her house, testing the limits of her invisibility. She waved her hand in front of her face, stared into the mirror, and even tiptoed outside, feeling the thrill of being unseen. But then a chilling thought crept in: *What if I can't turn back?*

Panic threatened to consume her, but she forced herself to stay calm. With a trembling finger, she clicked the pen again. She reappeared.

As the weight of this discovery settled over her, Emily realized the pen's power was both incredible and dangerous. She couldn't keep it a secret forever. But who could she trust? What if someone tried to take it from her?

The pen's mysteries were far from revealed—and her journey had only just begun.

Days turned into weeks, and Emily couldn't stop thinking about the pen. Its power was intoxicating. It's a responsibility, exhausting.

It was just a simple ballpoint pen, completely unmarked except for a faint scratch where a logo might've been. The cap clicked shut perfectly, and the ink never seemed to run out—until the moment she needed it most.

She started carrying it everywhere.

One afternoon in the library, Emily noticed a group of young men whispering in the corner. Curiosity got the better of her. She clicked the pen—and vanished.

Invisible, she inched closer, straining to hear. They were discussing a string of thefts that had been plaguing the neighborhood markets. The ringleader, Jerome—a manipulative young man she remembered from school—was bragging about his latest heist.

Emily's heart raced. She had stumbled upon something profound. Determined to gather more, she began trailing Jerome.

She knew where he lived, and her hiding skills— honed during childhood games and lonely walks— served her well.

Although invisible, she had learned how to creep, how to blend into the shadows.

The next few days were a whirlwind of covert operations. Emily followed Jerome, documenting everything she could—from late-night meetings to stashes of stolen goods—while wrestling with the ethics of her actions. Emily thought, *"Should I report him? Can I do it without revealing myself? What if they find out about the pen?"*

One evening, while reviewing her notes, Emily heard a noise outside her window. She crept toward the curtain and peeked through. There he was— Jerome—lingering in the shadows with a sinister smirk on his face. She thought, *"Does he know? Did I mess up?"*

Her chest tightened. Panic surged through her veins, but her mind snapped into focus. She had to act. She couldn't hide anymore.

This time, she wouldn't be the unseen observer. This time, she would face him.

The next day, at the park, Emily approached Jerome with a pen in hand. He tried to intimidate her, brushing off her words with laughter and arrogance.

Until she clicked the pen and vanished.

The color drained from Jerome's face. Fear widened his eyes as he spun in place, whispering curses under his breath.

Emily's voice came from nowhere. "I've been watching. I know everything. Try something again, and I'll make sure you're exposed."

Defeated, Jerome had no choice but to back down.

Emily clicked the pen and reappeared, meeting his stunned gaze one last time before walking away.

In the days that followed, the neighborhood markets were finally free from theft. Jerome kept his distance, and for the first time in weeks, Emily felt a strange calm.

Neighbors still chatted over white picket fences. Kids still played in the parks. But Emily's world—behind the brave face—was slowly crumbling.

The pressure of being a silent guardian, her parents' growing distance, and the weight of secrets made her feel more invisible than ever, even without the pen.

Then came the final straw. She overheard her parents in the kitchen, voices low and weary. They were talking about splitting up—divorce. Her breath caught in her chest. She thought, *"How could they? Did I do something wrong? Can't they see I'm barely holding on?"*

Desperate to fix it, Emily reached for the pen—the one thing that had brought her adventure, distraction, and hope. She clutched it tightly, staring at a blank page, and thought, *"Maybe if I write a happy ending for them... maybe everything will be okay again."* But just as she scribbled the first sentence, the ink ran dry. Nothing happened. No vanishing. No change.

The pen was out of ink.

Emily stared at the empty page, heartbroken.

Tears blurred her vision as a quiet realization settled in: the pen had never truly held the power it seemed to. *It was just a tool.* It couldn't erase her problems or rewrite reality. It could only distract her from what was real.

She thought back on everything—Jerome, the thrill of hiding, the tension in her home, and now, the silence of her parents drifting apart. But something stirred in her chest, a whisper, a reminder. The thought was this: *The strength was never in the pen. It was in me.*

She had chosen to help. She had stood up to fear. She had faced the truth, even when it hurt.

In a quiet act of finality, Emily snapped the pen in half. The broken plastic pieces tumbled to the floor. It was over. She stood taller. No more hiding. No more illusions.

She crossed the room, opened her drawer, and pulled out a new pen—one without magic, mystery, or shortcuts—just ink and potential.

Sitting at her desk, she began to write, not to disappear, but to be seen, to tell her truth, and to create something real.

She decided to begin again—not as a girl with a disappearing pen, but as a young woman with a voice, a story, and a future.

THE FALLEN LEAF

I was at my worst. Nothing seemed to be going right, and I was struggling with my inner self, my surroundings, and my peace.

Each day brought more situations to add to the darkness surrounding me. Every day, I wished and prayed for the dark clouds to pass and for all the negativity to disappear.

I didn't realize how much I had been wounded over the years—or how many dead scars I had been carrying—until one day while sitting outside contemplating suicide, a leaf fell from the tree.

It landed in my lap.

"So, you, too, are tired of living," I said aloud as I gathered it in my hands. I continued, "I wish I could place you back on the stem so you could live forever

73

and enjoy the beauty and happiness you bring to others—but I can't."

So, I find myself talking to a leaf. Have I lost my mind?

"Sharing all my fears and worries with something that has no ears... or do they?" I said, shaking my head back and forth.

Nevertheless, I continued talking to it as if it were listening.

"Why did you fall from such a beautiful and strong tree? Are you in the same situation as I am? I wonder—do you and other things have emotions like we humans? Do you ever feel lonely, unworthy, afraid, abandoned, miserable, and used? Did you conclude that quitting was the best answer? Was falling from the tree your way of ending it all?"

As I paused from talking to the leaf, I began to think back to when it was just a bud waiting to bloom. Then I started to look at myself.

I, too, started as a seed—waiting for the moment of transformation, budding into something beautiful and being loved, nourished, cared for, supported, and enjoying life. That was my spring season.

Just like the leaves on the trees, we also have our seasons.

Now, it's beginning to change for both of us. We feel the coolness, the lack of laughter, the isolation. The brutality of people—yes, they slander and hit us with words. They slap or shake us, sometimes for no reason, and sometimes just because they can.

And if that's not enough, nature comes in with strong winds and blows us all over the place.

How can we survive this process? Are we even meant to survive?

Is this the death I spoke of earlier?

No—it's only the fall season of life.

And then there's ole man winter.

The winter season arrives, and it gets even colder outside. The warmth is gone. The ground becomes hard, sometimes covered in frost or snow. Soon enough, we're buried beneath weeds, thistles, and dirt, with snow and ice on top.

Why am I complaining? Isn't this what I said I wanted?

As the *ole* folks say, *"Be careful what you ask for. It's not always greener on the other side."*

As time took its course, I watched in amazement as the snow and cold eventually gave way, bringing forth a newness in the world. Dormant things began to bud again, awakened from sleep with more beauty and vitality, more joy and laughter, and more reason to live.

Our spring season has sprung into action.

And after spring comes summer, full of laughter, family outings, and reminiscing on old summers, early mornings, and late nights. And don't forget the heat.

And now I understand: The Seasons of Life.

During the fall, our old things, dead things, wounded things, broken things, and negativity are meant to fall off. With the onset of winter, God cleanses and plants new seeds in us to bear fruit. While dormant, the old and empty version of us is prepared to handle the next. Thankfully, we don't sleep too long— because, when in His care, we spring into action.

It's not easy, but guess what? We have the power to spring forward, jump over obstacles, and bounce back through our circumstances or situations.

As I look back, I will rejoice, loving the process I went through. After all, a new season is on the way.

A time of reflection, reunions, new friendships, and fun are on the way.

Fallen leaf, you must remember this: Sometimes it gets hard, overwhelming, and lonely, and you feel like giving up. However, remember that where you are now is not your final destination.

It is just a season.

And if you grasp the wisdom it dispels, you may just become that tree, planted firmly on a foundation not made by man. You will bear much fruit and leave a legacy of blessings behind.

And just think... You thought you were a fallen leaf, not knowing that you had seeds inside you that needed to be born.

And to do that...

You had to fall.

PART 3
REDEMPTION & PURPOSE

Now, we reach the part of the journey where the light begins to peek through.

These stories carry pieces of me that I used to keep hidden. But The Lord wouldn't let me stay quiet. I remember saying, *"This is different for me. I'm exposing myself. But God wants me to be more public with my worship."* And for me, writing is worship.

What you'll find here is not perfection—it's redemption. You'll meet women who fall, get back up, and discover that what almost broke them became the very thing God used to build them.

It's not about being seen by the world. It's about being seen by God and realizing you've been held the whole time.

I don't know what road you're on Today, but if you've ever asked, *"God, are you still with me?"* I hope these stories answer you loud and clear because, yes, He is. He is still with you.

HER NAME IS UU

After giving her life to God, she made a concerted effort to live by His Word. She read The Bible daily, prayed, worshiped, and praised God for all He did and continued to do in her life.

She had not a care in the world—because she trusted God completely (or so she thought).

One day, for no apparent reason, she began to feel a sense of loneliness. Depression tried to set in. Then along came her friend with answers to all her questions. She said all the right things (all lies), so she started to feel a little better.

She went out and bought a lotto ticket—and won. Now she's on cloud nine. Instead of Bible study, she's picking numbers, reading horoscopes, and buying get-rich books. Her Bible collects dust, and her praises turn into shouts, "I did it!"

She changes her style of dress, attracting all the wrong men, looking good on the outside but battling demons on the inside. She managed to turn some down, but there was *one that she couldn't*. You know—there's always one who can steal the cookie out of the cookie jar and the sweetness out of gingerbread.

She was in love. Or so she thought.

Her praises now went to her new man. Her prayer life became nonexistent. But she was happy—so she thought—in love with the man of her dreams. She was so in love that she would do anything for him.

Then, one day, he asked her to do him a favor.

He said, "Just this one time. Please, baby, please— you know I love you. This is for *us*. A lot of money is involved. Trust me."

She did the trick. Not only once, but over and over again—until she started taking drugs to forget the shame.

Now, Mr. Good-Looking Man had become Mr. Wife-Beater. Mr. Bad. Her pimp.

No more *us*—just *him*.

Still, she tried to win back his love, his heart, and that joy she felt the first time he made her feel special. In her mind, she was determined to make it work. She would stay out more hours, do more tricks—until he came to love her again.

All was well for a couple of days. She thought she had gotten her Prince Charming back.

Then, one day, she decided to surprise him. She had collected a bonus and wanted the two of them to celebrate like they used to in the old days. But to her surprise, when she returned home, the joy of uniting with her man turned into disaster.

She found her man in the arms of another woman.

She felt distraught, hurt, betrayed, broken, and used. The emptiness inside her gave her no reason to continue living. She thought of the gun he kept for protection—*to kill them both.* But that would mean jail for life, rehashing all the memories of pain and shame she now carried.

So, she put the gun to her head and said, "God, please forgive me."

And it was at that moment she had a flashback of what her life was like before she met the new friends, the money, and the "good man."

Still holding the gun to her head, she cried out:

"Where are my friends? Why am I all alone again, to face more pain?

Jesus, where are You? I remember Your Word said You will never leave me.

If You are here, Lord, I need Thee. Help me, for I have sinned—lost in a whirlwind, going nowhere."

She recalled more scriptures and began to recite them aloud to The Lord. With each breath she took, she was being strengthened, revived, restored, and renewed.

She placed the gun down and continued to pray.

The more she poured out her heart to God, the stronger she became.

She realized she was on a path to self-destruction, blinded by sin, false hope, money, and fake friends.

"Where did I go wrong?" she asked herself.

"I put more value in the creations than I did the Creator," she answered. (Romans 1:25)

She felt better about herself now. Her prayers grew more powerful as she continued to plead her case before The Lord, asking for forgiveness and another chance.

Tears—and more tears—rolled down her face, washing away the shame, the pain, the addiction, the depression, and the loneliness.

Lying in a fetal position, crying to her Father, she felt His presence, and a still voice said:

"I forgive you. Welcome home, my child."

HUMBLE BEGINNINGS

James Willard was an extraordinarily successful writer. He authored books covering all areas of life, many of which were turned into movies that became box office hits.

Coming from a small town in Alabama with only a high school education and no college degree, it was nothing short of a miracle that he had become so successful in life.

During his childhood, he would always confess to wanting to be a writer. He often told his teachers, "I want to be a writer when I grow up." But being a writer was no job for someone from a small town in Alabama. The only jobs available, at best, were farming, teaching at school, working as a store clerk, or serving in the café. There was simply no future for a writer in Aliceville, Alabama—the small town he called home.

But that did not change his mind. He loved to write. He wrote about farming, sunsets, blue skies, butterflies—whatever came to mind. Throughout his young life, his siblings and school peers laughed at him, made jokes, and distanced themselves from him. But James did not give up. He welcomed the alone time and continued to write. His parents, although they hoped he would take over the farm, supported him and his dream.

As time went on, James entered high school at the age of 16, and his writing was noticed.

Mrs. C. Davis, his English teacher, asked the class to write a two-page story about any subject of their choosing. Naturally, James was excited. He didn't need to write one from scratch—he could choose from the large stacks he had written over the years.

When it was time to hand in the assignment, Mrs. Davis was glad to see the participation of the entire class. The girls wrote about wanting to be mothers or store clerks. The boys wrote about jobs they wanted, their families, and military service. They were all delightful stories, but when she read James' story about the butterfly, her excitement reached another level.

James loved science, so he was able to explain the distinct stages of the butterfly and compare them to everyday life. As Mrs. Davis read the story, she realized that James truly had the makings of a writer. With every opportunity she had, she helped him with all aspects of writing—grammar, structure, and the use of nouns, pronouns, and commas.

The year before he finished high school, James worked for the local newspaper in his hometown. He saw spreading the news as a means of spreading joy, so he only printed happy stories and events, along with words of encouragement. After a couple of years, however, his boss wanted him to write about the good, the bad, and the ugly. But James couldn't see how spreading bad stories or disappointing news would bring happiness to his readers.

Although he was happy to have a job where he could share joy, love, and hope through his writing, he resigned at age 21—but continued to write.

James's boss, Mr. Harley, wasn't happy about the decision. He tried to explain to James that life was not all good news and that the newspaper had an obligation to keep people informed of all things. He emphasized the ups and downs of life and how people relied on the news to stay informed about what was happening around them. But James, having made up his mind, disagreed.

"I should start a paper of my own—just filled with good news, encouraging words, and love," was a thought that passed through James' mind.

He mentioned the idea to Mrs. Davis, his teacher, who understood him and was the one with whom he shared all his stories, but she wasn't as excited as he had expected. She knew James had more to offer, and she wouldn't let him settle for less. Determined to see his work published, she submitted story after story to publishing companies across the country. And time after time, they were rejected.

James spent his days writing about the beauty of nature and his surroundings. Little did he know that one piece—about the birds—would change his life.

To the naked eye, they were only birds. But to a writer with a flair for words, they became so much more. James had written pages of short stories since leaving the newspaper, and at the age of 25, he decided to share them with his friend and teacher, Mrs. Davis.

As always, Mrs. Davis was eager to read James's work. When he presented her with five folders of writing, she knew in her heart that one of them would be his ticket to recognition. As she read each story from cover to cover, it was the story about the birds that captured her attention.

Never before had she seen birds displayed in such a manner. Through the eyes of a writer whose words carried depth and meaning far beyond the ordinary, she was sure this would be a winner. And she was right.

Offers came in from all over the globe. Mrs. Davis was especially elated—but faced one dilemma: what would she tell James?

She knew he wasn't in it for the fame. He simply loved to write things that would make a difference in someone's life. But she also knew she had to explain why his stories needed to be published—to reach readers who needed hope, laughter, and joy.

With excitement in her heart, Mrs. Davis rode out to meet James and tell him the good news. But just half a mile from his home, while trying to avoid hitting a baby deer, she lost control of her car and landed in a ditch, killing her instantly.

The whole town mourned Mrs. Davis for days, but no one felt the heartache and brokenness that James felt. She was the one person who truly understood his passion for writing. He felt hurt and abandoned, too much pain for a young man of 25 to endure.

He blamed the accident on himself and his writing. He vowed never to draft another story. He became a recluse, which worried his parents. He wasn't sleeping, eating, or writing.

Then, one day, he went for a walk in the woods, questions swirling in his mind.

He asked himself, "Why did she have to die because of me? Why? What can I do? What have I done?"

So much pain, grief, and sorrow lay buried in his heart. He wanted to die.

Call it a dream or a vision, but his own words came back to him from the story about the butterfly's metamorphosis—the various stages of growth into beauty, into freedom.

At that moment, he understood what Mrs. Davis had been trying to do. He understood why his boss had told him to write about both the good and the bad.

Dreadful things happen to us to grow and make us strong. Good things are joy and reward.

To honor her, he began to write again—and write he did. This time, he explored all subjects. And with each subject, he gained fame, respect, and recognition.

His life had just begun to take on purpose and meaning. He no longer thought of himself as the bearer of good tidings but as a man whose mission was to write—and to write to all about all things. From education and life challenges to happiness and pain—All could be experienced simply by turning a page.

And though the world would one day know him as James Willard, the acclaimed author, there would always be one name whispered in the quiet of his heart: Mrs. Davis.

Each story he published was dedicated to her, not with ink, but with intent.

He often said, "If my words ever lift a burden, brighten a day, or make someone feel seen, then she still lives."

Whenever he rose in the morning to write, in the silence of early morning with pen and paper in hand, he would pause, smile gently, and whisper, *"This is for you, Mrs. Davis."*

DEALING WITH THE DIRT

My name is Nefertiti—a powerful and beautiful queen with a strong will and ideas no man has ever claimed.

Throughout my life, I have allowed my beauty and power to be overshadowed by all the turmoil I have endured while dealing with family, friends, and foes.

The negative words, the mockery, the shame, the loneliness, the betrayal, and the isolation—each one a shovel of dirt thrown at me daily until I am completely covered.

The original beauty, the uniqueness of the person God made me to be, is now layered over with dirt. And the more I wiggle and try to shake it off, the more something else is said or done that keeps me buried.

So, I have learned to exist by using this dirt as a fortress. I will not let anyone get near me. Many have come close, but no one has entered.

How long must I stay in this fortress—this dark hole covered with dirt—is a question with no answer. For now, it feels safe. I am still me. But deep down, I know this is not who or where God wants me to be.

Where can I go to escape the hurt, the harshness, and the pain? Who will rescue me from the loneliness, dig me out of this dark hole, and restore my self-worth?

I am Nefertiti—a powerful, beautiful, resilient queen—and I will be the diamond I am destined to be.

So, while I remain in this dark place where others say I am nothing, I am reminded of the process of the diamond and how we both have something in common. It, too, is buried in a dark place. It is unique, valuable, beautiful, strong, and resilient—formed under pressure and heat over millions of years, deep within the earth, to become a priceless gem.

I, too, will grow from the challenges and difficult circumstances I am forced to endure. I am unique, possessing the traits, experiences, and perspectives that make me a valuable individual. My imperfections contribute to my individuality and beauty.

Diamonds symbolize purity, love, and eternal commitment—all I long for in this life. Diamonds go through a transformation process. I am going through one right now. It requires effort, learning, and self-improvement.

Diamonds are mined. People or machines must dig deep into the earth to uncover this priceless treasure. So now, must I, too, wait until someone comes to uncover me? I did not choose to be covered with dirt and buried deep in a dark place, but it was necessary to bring out the true value of my worth.

I am not coming out the same way I went in.

I am Nefertiti—a queen: beautiful, strong, priceless, rare, and precious—bringing uniqueness to the world.

The process is not always easy, but it is necessary.

Can you handle the dirt?

ABOUT THE AUTHOR
SUSIE KIRK-BONES

Susie Kirk-Bones is a child of God, an author, and a retired transit worker whose pen flows with reflections on faith, family, and the quiet strength found in life's everyday moments. A lifelong dreamer, Susie finds her inspiration in the beauty of nature, the truths of The Scripture, and the ordinary people who carry extraordinary stories.

Born and raised in a close-knit community, Susie's heart has always been drawn to storytelling that heals, restores, and uplifts. Her writing captures the warmth of porch conversations, the sting of hard lessons, and the grace that shows up even in the darkest seasons. Whether through personal testimony, fictional tales, or poetic reflections, her voice offers comfort, insight, and deep-rooted hope.

Now retired, Susie embraces a life filled with long walks, peaceful mornings, and time spent meditating by the water's edge. She enjoys reading, writing plays, singing old hymns, and cherishing moments with her husband Joseph, son Anthony, and a circle of beloved family and friends.

Echoes of the Journey is her debut collection of short stories—some true, some imagined, all crafted with a tender honesty that reminds readers they are never alone, never forgotten, and always part of a greater story.

Susie continues to write from her home, fueled by faith and a commitment to encourage others. She looks forward to sharing more stories and poems that reflect God's enduring love and the beauty found in brokenness, redemption, and everyday grace.

Susie Kirk-Bones, a.k.a Susie "Q"

I would love for you to stay connected with me as I continue my journey of ministry and writing. Follow, engage, and keep in touch through email:

Email: For personal inquiries or ministry updates, reach out via email: SusieKirk3@aol.com

THANK YOU FOR READING!

I hope this book has blessed, inspired, and impacted your life. Your feedback is incredibly important, and I'd love to hear from you!

Leave a Review and 5-Star Rating

How to Leave a Review on Amazon

1. Go to the book's page on **Amazon** (search for the title or author).

2. Scroll down to the **Customer Reviews** section.

3. Click on **"Write a Customer Review."**

4. Select the number of stars and write your feedback.

5. Click **Submit**—and that's it!

Thank you for being so supportive. Your feedback can help others find this book and experience the same impact.

May GOD continue to bless and guide you on your journey.